SCRATCH AND SPARKLE

MERMAIDS
Activity Book

Dive into the magical world of mermaids
in this sparkling activity book!

Use your favorite pens and pencils to complete
the activities. Then go to the back of the book
to create rainbow models and dazzling crafts.

From a mermaid lagoon model to a glittering
tiara, there are hours of fun to be had!

make
believe
ideas

How to use your scratch-off pages:

At the back of the book, there are mermaid crafts for you to press out, create, and wear. Look for the instructions on the activity pages to see what you can make.

1. Use the scratcher to add sparkling details.

2. Gently press out the shapes.

3. Finish with ribbon, glue, and some help from an adult!

Craft content

Mermaid Lagoon
See page 5

Clam purse
See page 11

Mermaid tiara
See page 15

Mix-and-match mermaids
See page 19

Bobbing fish
See page 23

Mermaid necklace
See page 25

Meet the mermaids

Find the mermaids that look like these.

3

Mermaid Lagoon

Search the lagoon for the things below. How many can you see? Write the answers in the circles.

2 ...... pearls

...... seahorses

...... crabs

...... purple shells

...... dolphin

...... mermaids

...... jellyfish

...... mirrors

MAKE YOUR OWN MERMAID LAGOON

1. Use your scratcher to add colorful details to the lagoon shapes.

2. Gently press out the lagoon shapes and open the slots.

3. Slot the big piece onto the little piece to make it stand up.

Mermaid mix-up

Find the thing that doesn't belong in each group.

6

fishy friends

Guide the mermaid through the maze to the finish. Collect all the fish along the way.

Start

Finish

How many fish did you collect? Write the answer.

7

Tail twins

Circle the one pair of identical friends.

Ocean rows

Which row of ocean animals matches the silhouette below?

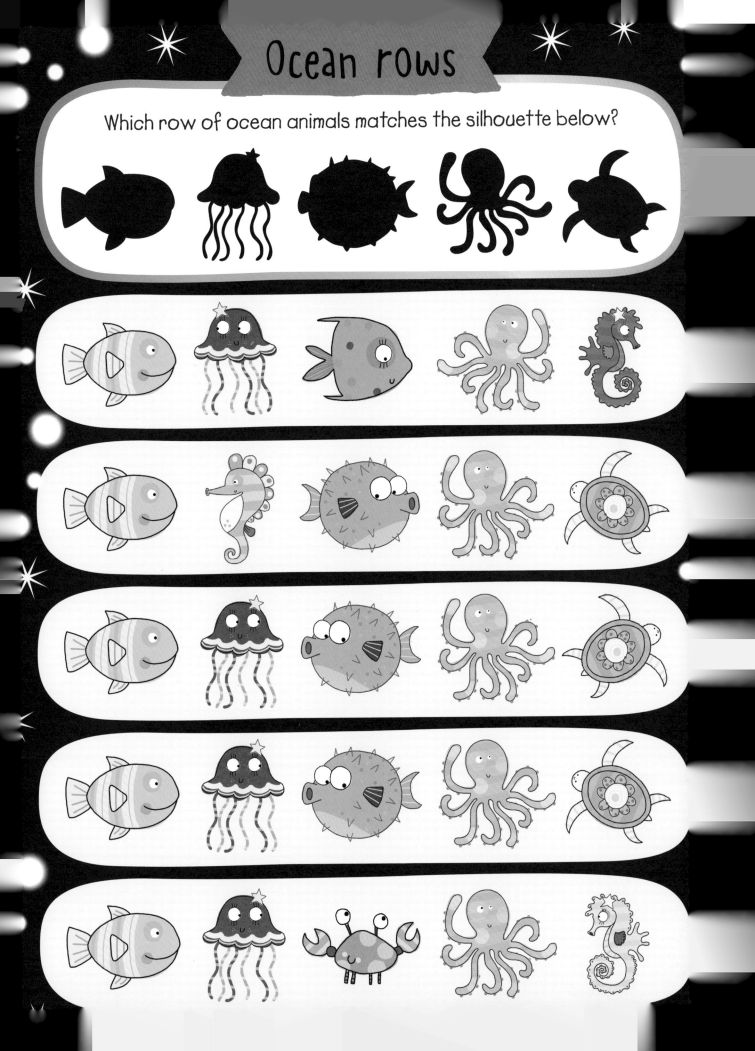

Under the sea

Find and color...

a spotted octopus, yellow.

a merman wearing a crown, blue.

a mermaid holding a bag, pink.

a jellyfish with six legs, purple.

Then color the other pictures to finish.

MAKE YOUR OWN CLAM PURSE

1. Use your scratcher to add dazzling details to the purse and charm shapes.

3. Tape the tabs to the inside of the purse. Now press out the charms.

2. Gently press out the purse shape and fold along the creases.

4. Ask an adult to help you thread them on some ribbon, and then tie the ribbon to the purse to finish.

11

Rock 'n' roll

Use the clues to find out who wants to be a rockstar.

CLUE 1: The mermaid has a blue tail.

CLUE 2: The mermaid is wearing headphones.

CLUE 3: The mermaid has purple hair.

Selina

Rey

Alyssa

Sasha

Britney

Cara

Who wants to be a rockstar? Write the name.

Sparkle spots

Search the grid for the patterns below.
Check the boxes when you've found them.

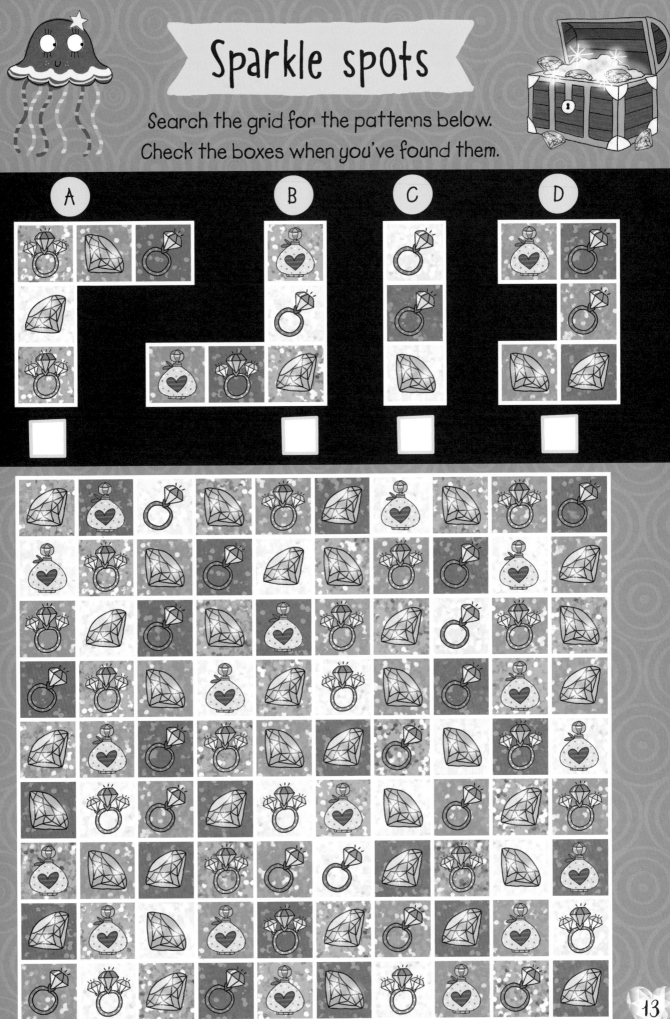

A
B
C
D

1 crown ☐

1 spear ☐

2 earrings ☐

2 tiaras ☐

4 wands ☐

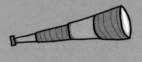

6 telescopes ☐

10 gems ☐

14

Treasure hunt

Search the scene for the lost treasures.
Check the boxes when you find them.

MAKE YOUR OWN MERMAID TIARA

1. Use your scratcher to add colorful details to the tiara.

2. Gently press out the tiara shape and small holes either side.

3. Ask an adult to help you thread some ribbon through the holes and tie it around your head.

Friends forever

Join the dots to finish the mermaids. Then color them in.

My mermaid name

Circle the first letter of your name.

F – Shelly

G – Aqua

A – Melody

H – Coral

B – Ariel

I – Delphin

C – Zelda

J – Serena

D – Venus

K – Jewel

E – Azalea

L – Luna

M – Amatheia

N – Meri

O – Nixie

P – Oona

Q – Pearl

R – Calypso

S – Marina

T – Dominique

U – Sandy

V – Faridah

W – Nerida

X – Muriel

Y – Imogen

Z – Isla

Circle the month you were born.

January – Ocean

February – Bubble

March – Moon

April – Seaflower

May – Gemhold

June – Shore

July – Shimmer

August – Starburst

September – Storm

October – Sparkle

November – Glimmer

December – Gillyweed

My mermaid name is:

....

....

Write your mermaid name on the badge. Then cut it out, ready to wear!

Beautiful bakes

Trace the lines to finish the chef hats.

Decorate the cakes and sweet toppings with doodles and color.

Find a pink whisk.

Find all the ingredients in the grid below.
Words can go across or down.

butter

cherries

chocolate

eggs

flour

sugar

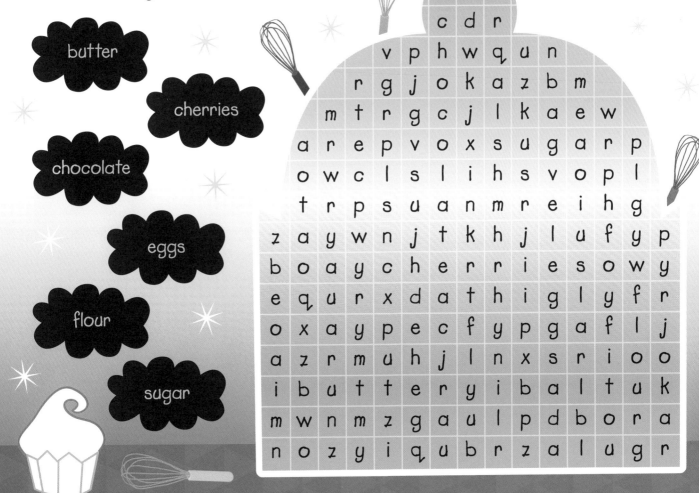

```
        a e b
        c d r
    v p h w q u n
  r g j o k a z b m
m t r g c j l k a e w
a r e p v o x s u g a r p
o w c l s l i h s v o p l
t r p s u a n m r e i h g
z a y w n j t k h j l u f y p
b o a y c h e r r i e s o w y
e q u r x d a t h i g l y f r
o x a y p e c f y p g a f l j
a z r m u h j l n x s r i o o
i b u t t e r y i b a l t u k
m w n m z g a u l p d b o r a
n o z y i q u b r z a l u g r
```

MAKE YOUR OWN MIX-AND-MATCH MERMAIDS

1. Use your scratcher to add colorful details to the mermaid and tail shapes.

2. Gently press out the mermaid shapes, tail shapes, and small holes.

3. Choose a mermaid and tail. Ask an adult to help you thread some ribbon through the holes and tie the tail to the mermaid.

4. Have fun making different mermaids! Move their tails up and down to make them swim in the mermaid lagoon.

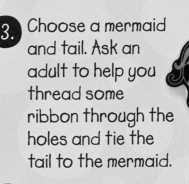

flower power

Who has the most flowers? Count the flowers for
each mermaid, and then write the totals in the spaces below.

Mer-maze

Find the path to the treasure. Use the key to guide you.

Key:

Sandcastle competition

Trace the lines to finish the sandcastle. Then color it in.

Finish the trophy.

Who matches this silhouette?

Find the thing that doesn't belong.

MAKE YOUR OWN BOBBING FISH

1. Use your scratcher to add rainbow details to the fish.

2. Gently press out the shapes and open the slots around the fish heads.

3. Fold along the crease to make them stand up.

4. Add them to your lagoon scene!

Sea scramble

Unscramble the words. Use the pictures as a guide.

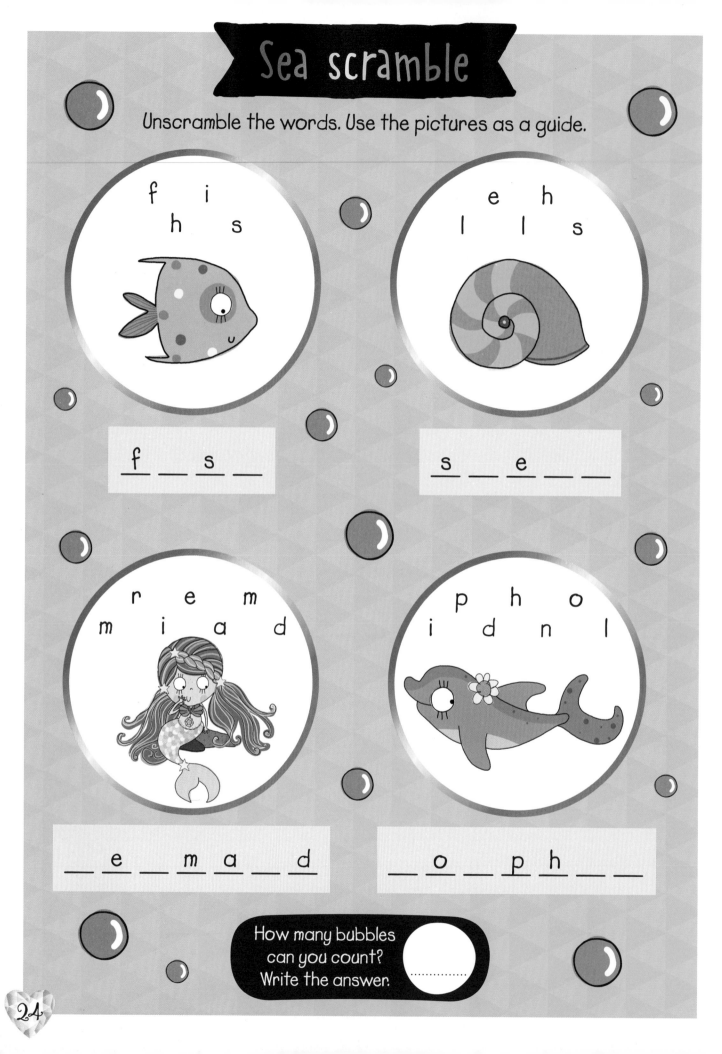

f i
h s

e h
l l s

f _ s _

s _ e _ _

r e m
m i a d

p h o
i d n l

_ _ e _ m _ a _ d

_ _ o _ p h _ _ _

How many bubbles can you count? Write the answer. ....

Amazing accessories

Draw lines to match each character to the correct colored accessory.

MAKE YOUR OWN MERMAID NECKLACE

1. Use your scratcher to add sparkling details to the necklace.

2. Gently press out the necklace and small holes at either end.

3. Ask an adult to help you thread some ribbon through the small holes and tie it around your neck.

Rush hour

Find ten differences between the busy scenes.